This Book Belongs To:

Gaze at Heaven above —
See sun, moon and stars.
Glance at those near;
You may see an angel.

~ Linda J. Hawkins

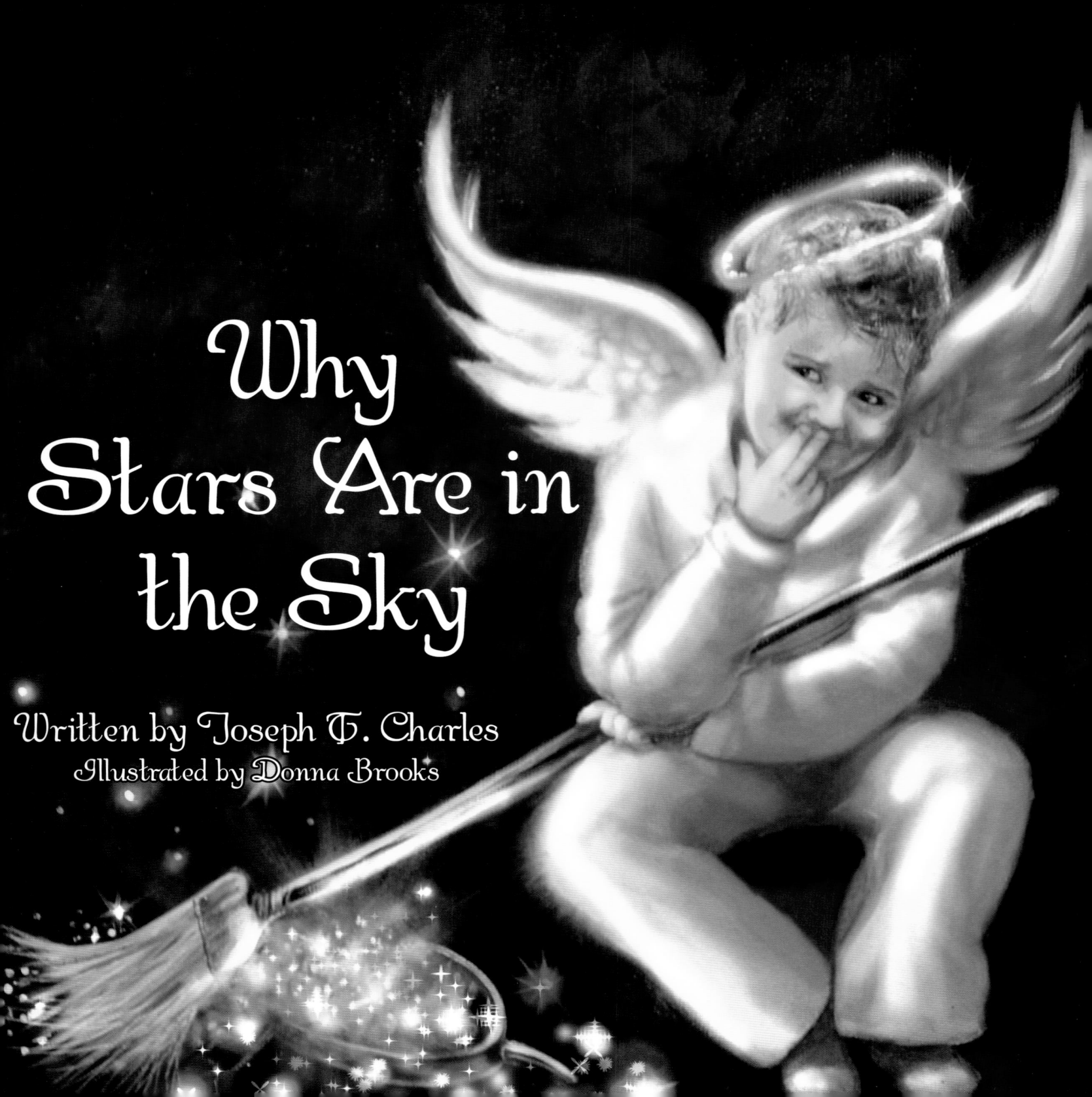

Why Stars Are in the Sky

Written by Joseph T. Charles

Illustrated by Donna Brooks

Heart to Heart   Publishing, Inc.

Heart to Heart Publishing, Inc,
528 Mud Creek Road • Morgantown, KY 42261
(270) 526-5589
www.hearttoheartpublishinginc.com

Title: Why Stars Are in the Sky
ISBN: 978-1-937008-00-0
Library of Congress 2010942798
Copyright 2010

Editor: Evelyn Byers
Copy-Editor: L. J. Gill
Artist: Donna Brooks
Designer: April Yingling

1 0 9 8 7 6 5 4 3 2

Printed and Bound March 2011, Nansha, Guangdong,China by Everbest Printing Company,Ltd. through Four Colour Imports,Ltd., Louisville, KY.

Heart to Heart books are available at a special discount for bulk purchases for fund raising efforts, sales promotions or educational use. Author and Illustrator available for book signings. Contact Heart to Heart Publishing for more information. Fax: (270) 526-7489

For Nina

~ Joseph T. Charles

I dedicate this book to my wonderful
husband, Billy Joe Woolsey,
my diamond in the rough!

~ Donna Brooks

Have you ever wondered why stars are in the sky? Some think they are twinkling lights that sparkle in the night sky. Others say stars are other suns like ours, but far, far away, so they look smaller than our sun. Could it be that there might be another reason? Let's read and see.

The sky is the bottom of Heaven where God and His angels live. On the beginning of time, when the Lord was making everything, He had only six days. Just think of all the work He had to do! Making something as important as the earth or as big as the sun must be done right the first time.

So the Lord called His angels together--tall ones and short ones, large ones and small ones, old ones and young ones, straight-haired ones and curly-haired ones.

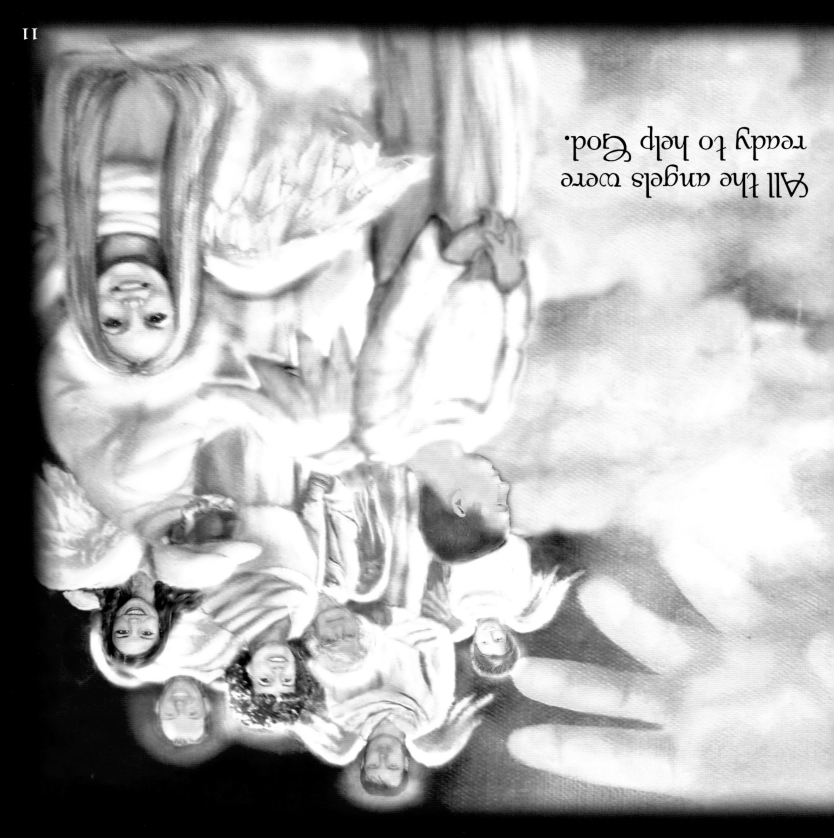

All the angels were
ready to help God.

On the day the sun was to be created, the angels- tall ones and short ones, large ones and small ones, old ones and young ones, straight-haired ones and curly-haired ones -- asked many questions about how the sun should be made.

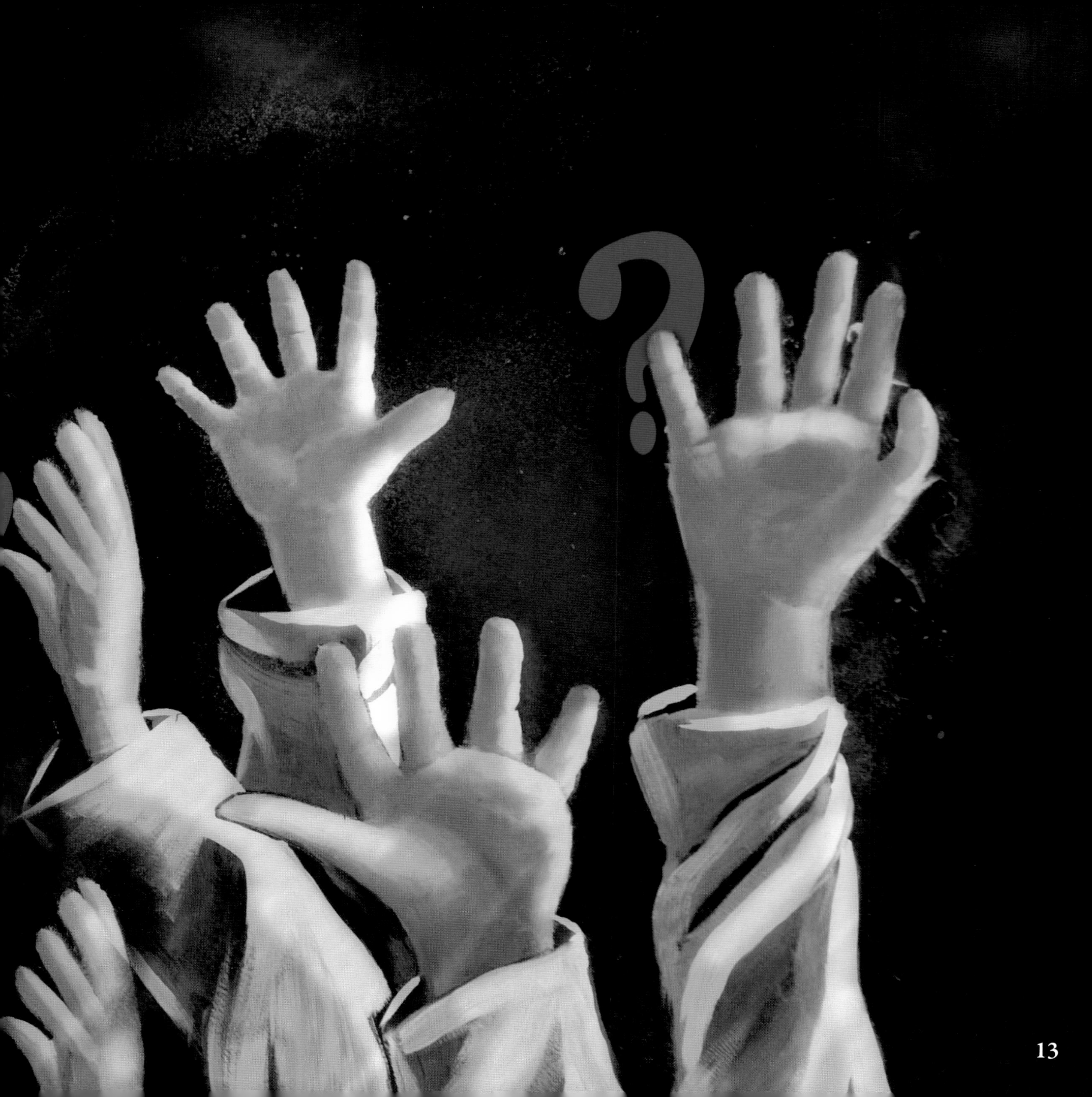

One smiling angel asked God,
"Should the sun be square or round?"

God's finger drew a circle in the air
and He said, "Round."

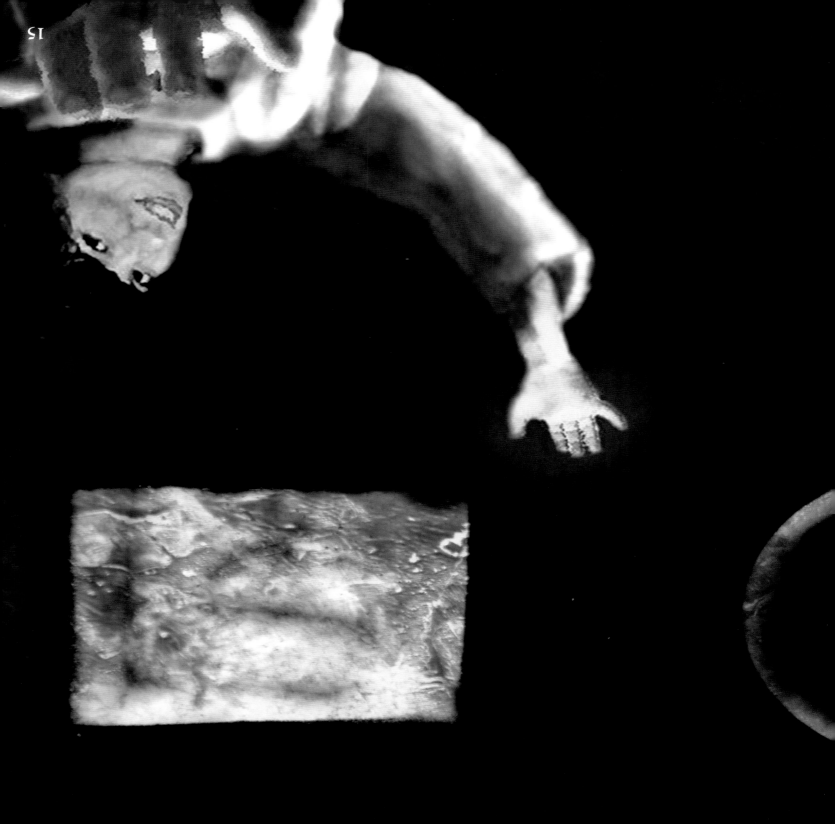

An older angel asked God, "Should the sun be small or large?"

God spoke softly, "It should be large, but made to look small by moving it far away from the earth."

A younger angel asked God,
"Should the sun be hot or cold?"

God answered, "Make the sun hot,
but not too hot, so all that live on the earth
will feel its warmth, yet not be burned."

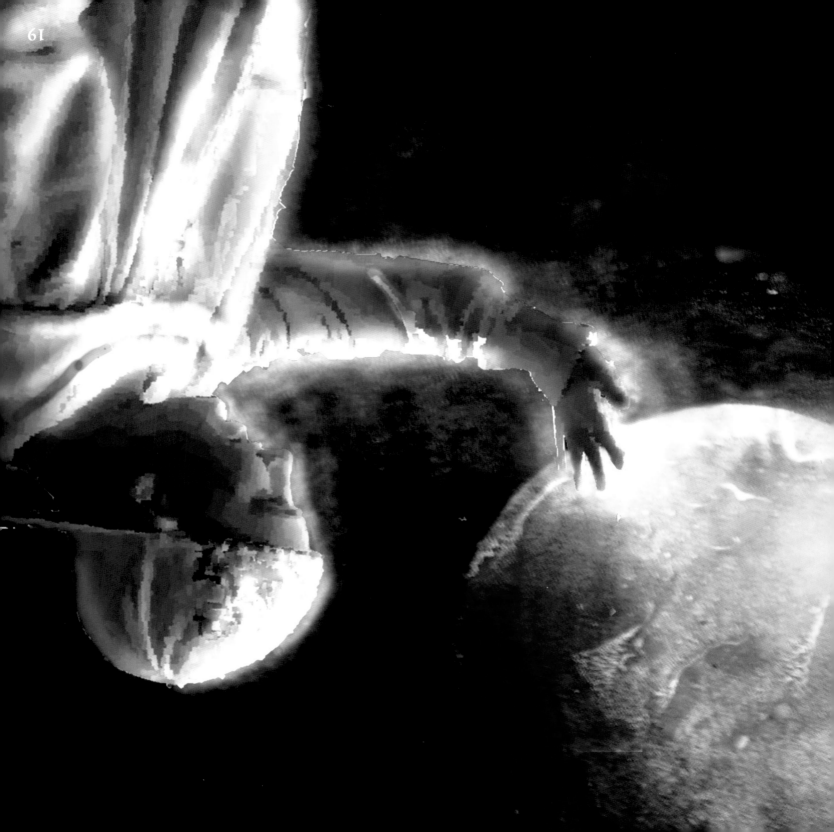

The Lord said, "Make it very bright so all who
see the sun will look toward the Earth and be
reminded how life is given to all that grows."

Then two angels with curly hair asked,
"How bright should the sun be?"

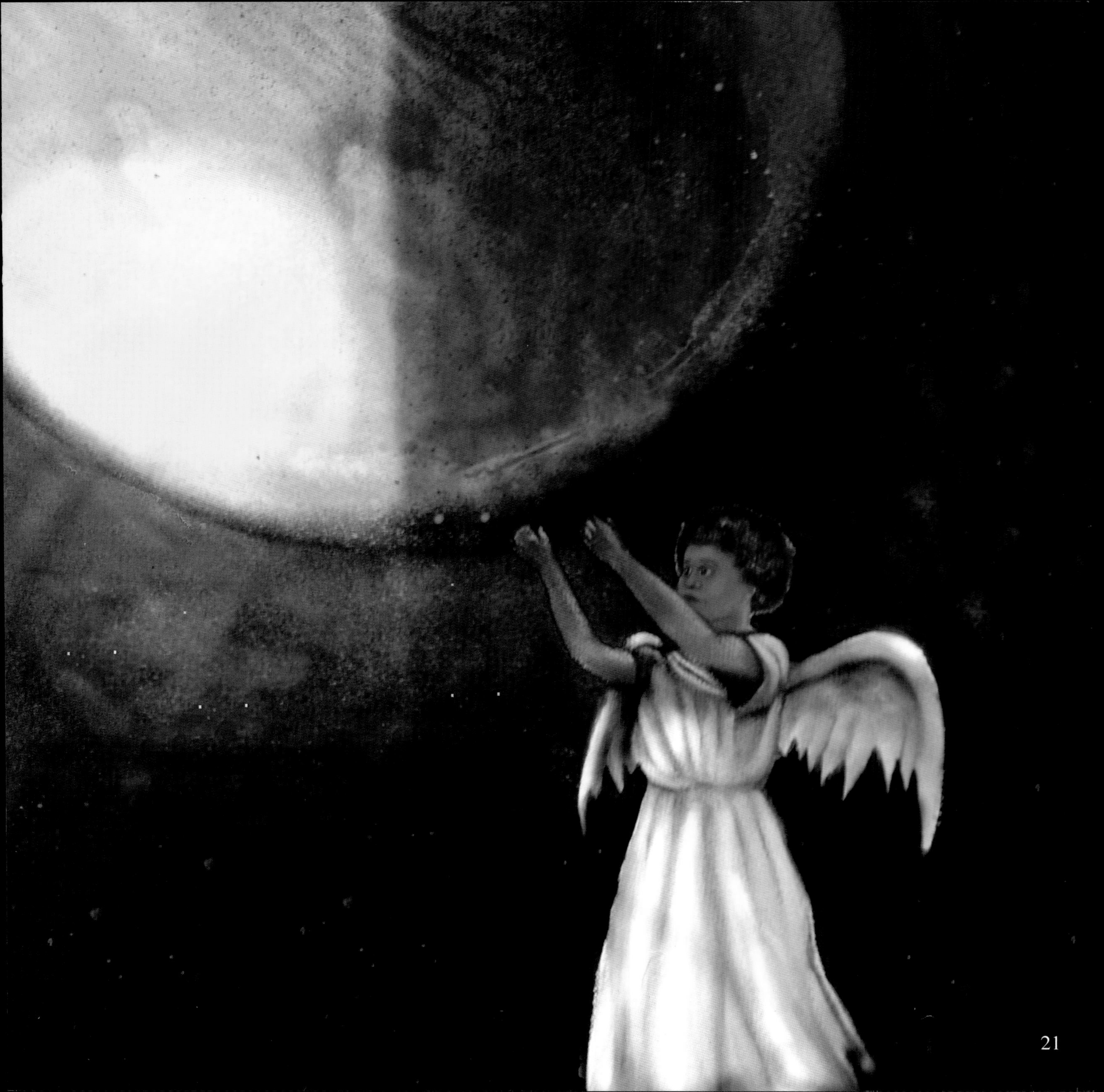

These Angels looked around for others who would
follow God's orders, but they were all busy doing
other work for The Lord. Then they saw
a small angel who wanted to help.

They said to each other.
"Well, it's a big job,
but he wants to try."

They handed him a little tray of sunlight and said,
"Pour this on top of the sun to make it brighter."
The small angel wanted to show that he could do
the work faster, so, he changed the little
tray of sunlight for a really large tray.

Up, up, up the long ladder he climbed, looking like a waiter carrying a huge tray of dishes. On the last step, he lost his balance on the ladder leading to the sun. The large tray of sunlight flew from his hands and bits of sunlight spilled through the air, finally landing on top of the sky.

When this happened, the small angel became very worried. God had not told the angels to put drops of sunlight on top of the sky. Quickly he found a broom and dustpan and began to sweep up the mess.

But it was too late. The other angels had noticed, and so had the Lord. The angels stopped their work.

Bits of sunlight were scattered over the sky.

"WHO DROPPED THESE BITS OF
LIGHT ON HEAVEN'S FLOOR?"

This voice was like thunder.

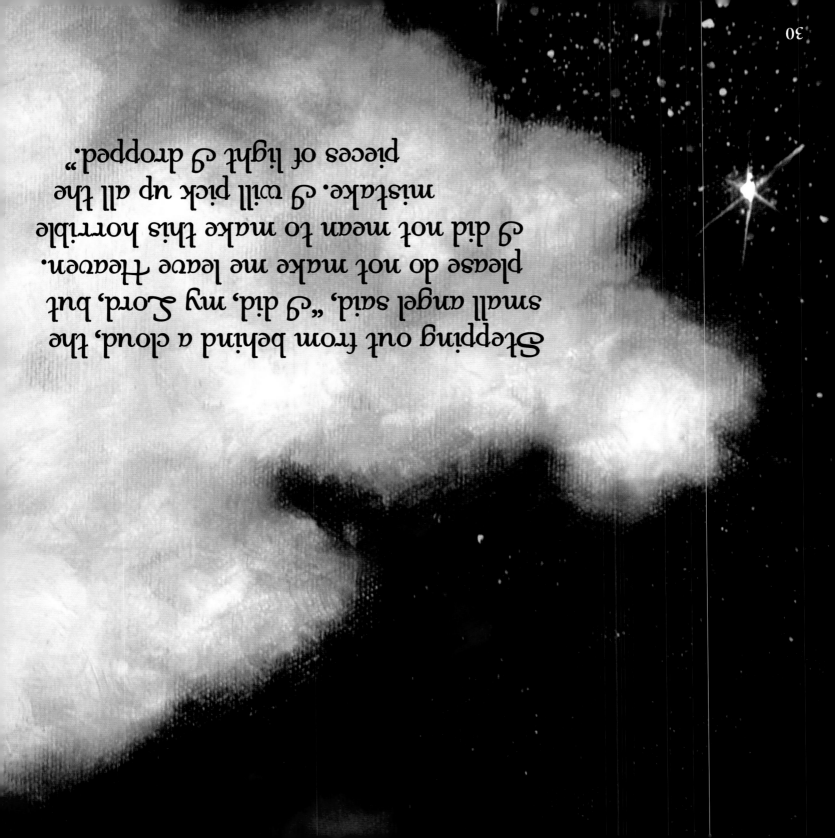

Stepping out from behind a cloud, the small angel said, "I did, my Lord, but please do not make me leave Heaven. I did not mean to make this horrible mistake. I will pick up all the pieces of light I dropped."

The Lord smiled and said,
"Everyone look at this wonder that
has been created. It is a beautiful
mistake, small angel. You have
scattered bright drops of sunlight
across the sky. Do not clean them up."

The Lord gathered all the angels in Heaven together and proclaimed, "All these beautiful drops of sunlight will now and forever be known as stars."

The Lord pointed to the small angel and said, "Sometimes honest mistakes happen for a reason. Small angel, you will have a job in Heaven. You are to polish these stars and make sure they always sparkle at night."

All the angels clapped their hands and shouted,
"Hooray!"

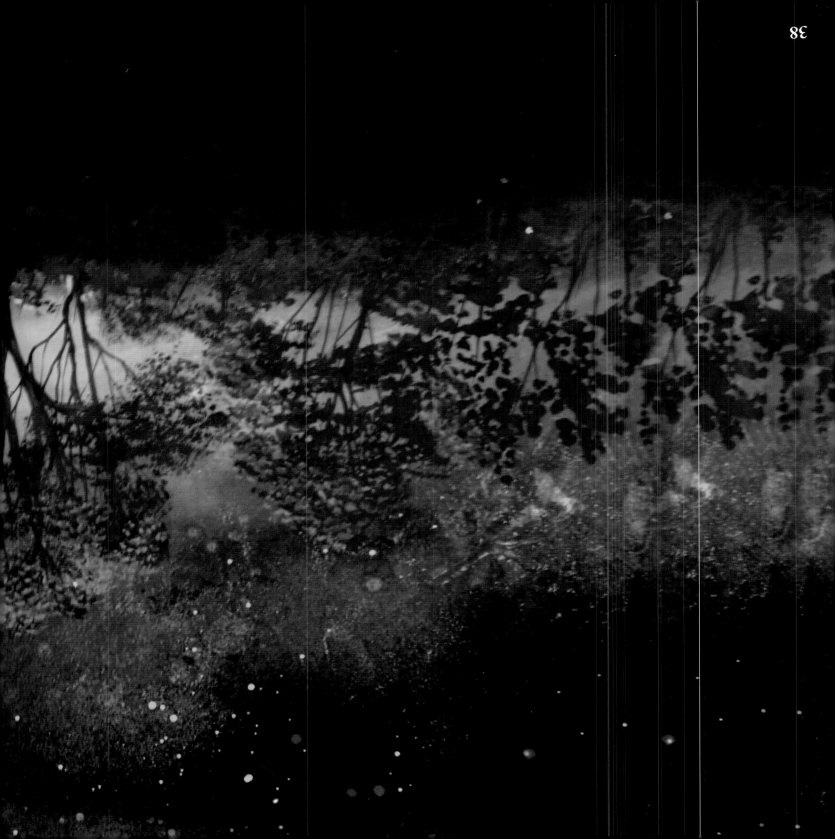

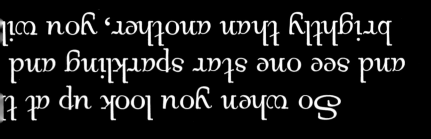

So when you look up at t

and see one star sparkling and

brightly than another, you wil

We

Thank You

s who have received their wings:
dréa Bernadette Coleman
Chuck Blanchett
reat Grandma C.Rogers
Letitia Melton Syler
Lista Syler McCully
bert Myles Cunningham
anda J.Blanchett Miller

ur earthly angel models:
Brooks, Andrew Kyle Gill,
rrett Poole, Deana Uzzle,
Joe Woolsey